Angela McAllister

WINTER'S CHILD

ILLUSTRATED BY

Grahame Baker-Smith

templar publishing

IT WAS the
longest winter Nana
could remember.

Each morning she brushed
the snow from her window box,
waiting for a tiny green shoot,
a sign of spring.

BUT TOM loved the winter.
All day he skated on the lake and sledged on the hill.
At night he dried his wet gloves and boots by the fire.

"I wish winter could go on forever!" he sighed.

Tom's mother was pleased to see him happy,
but she was worried about Nana.

"It's been too cold, too long, for an old woman,"
she muttered one morning as she tied Tom's scarf.
"Nana needs the spring sun."

TOM FETCHED his skis
and set off across the white meadow.

He looped and swooped,
making spray sparkle
in the crisp cold air.

OUT OF the snow stepped a pale boy with ice-blue eyes.
Tom stopped and smiled.

"Do you want to play?" asked the boy. "Yes," said Tom.

The boy ran off and Tom followed.

They found a secret valley deep in drifted snow.
Tom and the boy made polar bears and arctic hares and dazzling white horses.

"I want winter to go on forever!"
cried the boy.

They played all day until
Tom heard his mother calling him home.

"I have to go," he said sadly.

"Goodbye," said the boy. "Let's play tomorrow."

THAT NIGHT, as Tom
gazed out at the starry winter world,
he heard a distant voice call from the mountains.
But he didn't see the pale figure sitting
beneath his window.

Outside, the boy put his hands
over his ears and curled up tight.

NEXT DAY,

there were only
four logs left in
the woodshed.

"What will we do?" Tom's mother sighed.
"If the spring sun doesn't come soon,
how will we keep Nana warm?"

Tom went out and chopped up his wooden skis for firewood.
"I'm too old for these now," he told Nana.

Then Tom went out to play.

THE BOY was waiting.

He took Tom to a forest
where glistening icicles hung like chimes.
"Look, we can make winter music," he said.
Together, they filled the snow-hushed air with tinkling notes.

Animals and birds crept
out of the forest to listen.

"Do you hear a sad voice calling?" asked Tom.
But the boy shook his head.

NEXT DAY there was no more firewood.
Tom chopped up the ladder to his treehouse.
"I'm big enough to climb up the tree myself, now,"
he told Nana.

Tom's mother took the last vegetables
from the store cupboard to make hot soup for Nana.
"If only this long winter would end," she sighed.
"How can I plant seeds in this frozen earth?"

Tom went out to play. Once more, the boy was waiting.

The snow was criss-crossed with hoof prints.
Tom and the boy followed the tracks until they found a reindeer stag.

The boy climbed gently onto the reindeer's back
and pulled Tom up behind him.
With a snort of frosty breath, the reindeer galloped off
and carried them to a ravine of frozen waterfalls.

TOM AND the boy played
in and out of the waterfalls all day…

until it was time to ride home.

"WHERE DO you live?"
Tom asked the boy as they neared his house.
"Everywhere and nowhere," laughed the boy, and then he was gone.

That night there was nothing to burn on the fire.
Tom laid his wet gloves and boots by the cold hearth,
then he gave Nana all the blankets.

In the morning there was nothing for breakfast
because there was no fire to bake bread.
"Nana is thin as a reed and grey as ash,"
whispered Tom's mother.

Tom went out to play in his wet boots and gloves.

The boy was waiting.

"Let's play!" he said.
Tom made a pile of snowballs
but his heart was heavy.

"WHAT'S WRONG?" asked the boy.

Tom told him about his Nana.

"The winter has been too long for her," he said.

"She needs the warm spring sun."

The boy looked sad. He gazed at a shadow

slipping among the trees.

"I thought you wanted winter to last forever?"

But Tom shook his head. His feet were frozen
in his wet boots and he had no supper to go home to.
"See you tomorrow," he said.

That evening a pale face peered in through
the cottage window, but nobody noticed.
The boy turned away.

Inside, Nana beckoned Tom close.
"Fetch the window box to burn," she said.
"I'll never see a green shoot grow there."

Tom looked sadly at the empty window box.
To his surprise, he noticed fresh footprints
in the snow beneath.

TOM RAN out
into the moonlight.
The boy was walking away
over the fields.

"Wait," called Tom.
"Where are you going?"

"It's time I went home," said the boy.

"It's my fault that winter has been so long."

Tom was puzzled. "I don't understand."

"I am Winter's Child," said the boy.

"Spring cannot wake until Winter

and his child are asleep."

TOM STARED at his friend in wonder.

"I strayed away from my father because I wasn't ready to sleep,"
explained the boy. "I wanted the winter to last forever,
but I have played too long."

Tom looked around at the white, moonlit world.
"Winter *is* wonderful," he said.
"So is having a friend," said the boy.
Starlight sparkled in his ice-blue eyes. "I saw what you gave your Nana,
now I can give *you* something – I can give you spring."

"How will you
get home?" asked Tom.
The boy smiled. "My father
will fetch me if I call."
"Will you come back next year?"
"With the first snowflake!"
promised the boy.

TOM WALKED home.

He watched from his window as Winter's Child called for his father.

Suddenly, a fierce wind shook the trees. There was a thunder of hooves.

Out of the frozen air swirled a blizzard of snowflakes and Winter came,

riding a sleigh of ice. And the boy was gone.

NEXT MORNING Tom woke to the sound of dripping water.

The sun was shining and the world had already begun to thaw.
A tiny green shoot pushed through the earth in Nana's window box.

Tom looked up at the white-capped mountain.

"Sleep well, Winter's Child," he said.

"I'll be waiting.

When the snow returns, we'll play

TOGETHER AGAIN."